GETTING TO ROOM TEMPERATURE

GETTING TO ROOM TEMPERATURE

A HARD-HITTING, SENTIMENTAL AND FUNNY ONE-PERSON PLAY ABOUT DYING. BASED ON A MOSTLY TRUE STORY.

BY ARTHUR MILNER

GETTING TO ROOM TEMPERATURE

A hard-hitting, sentimental and funny one-person play about dying. Based on a mostly true story.

iUniverse books may be ordered through booksellers or by contacting:

iUniverse
1663 Liberty Drive
Bloomington, IN 47403
www.iuniverse.com
1-800-Authors (1-800-288-4677)

ISBN: 978-1-4917-9866-9 (sc)
ISBN: 978-1-4917-9868-3 (e)

Print information available on the last page.

iUniverse rev. date: 06/25/2016

PREFACE

I learned dramaturgy* from Patrick McDonald in the '80s, when he was artistic director of Ottawa's Great Canadian Theatre Company (GCTC) and I was resident playwright.

Sometime later, during Steven Bush's tenure as GCTC artistic director, Patrick was invited to lead a workshop of my new, one-person play, *Masada*. We gathered at the National Arts Centre's Atelier theatre. Gil Osborne, who ran the Atelier, was there, along with Steven, Patrick and me, and Robert Bockstael, who performed. Robert was maybe a third of the way through reading, when Patrick tossed the script into a trashcan. Steven and Gil were appalled; but Robert and I had worked with Patrick for years.

I admitted the play was, well, "a bad magazine article," but suggested we proceed nonetheless. Patrick shrugged and Robert continued.

The doorbell rang. Patrick volunteered to answer and headed down the hall, returning a minute later with two policemen. The bigger one,

---

* Dramaturgy is what playwrights call editing. Dramaturges, in North America, offer advice to playwrights. In Europe, dramaturgy is something else.

vii

an enormous man in a very shiny uniform, looked us over: "Which one of you is the playwright?"

"I am."

"You're under arrest for bad playwriting."

Robert raised his right hand: "I'll testify."

When we told that story afterwards, we described it as "GCTC Dramaturgy." I don't necessarily recommend the method to others.

Fifteen years later, I wrote a master's thesis on *avant garde* theatre. (I'd be very happy if you read it.) I quoted from one of my favourite critics, Eric Bentley:

> What offers itself as theater must submit to be judged as theater and not appeal to a higher court. ... Respect for an art means respect for the medium through which that art functions; the limitations of the medium are happily accepted, not combated or ignored. ... The critic of theatre must be permitted to say when a work bursts the theater's bounds, as ... political theater [is] clearly tempted to do (*In Search of Theatre*, 1953).

There are different approaches to dramaturgy. My preference is the dramaturge who, for a start, is a little embarrassed by the word, and who notices and is ready to state the obvious — like the critic of carpentry who will point out, "That table is going to fall over."

*　　*　　*

My mother was ninety-three and a half and quite healthy when she took a turn for the worse. I accompanied her to the doctor, who asked, "What can I do for you?"

My mother said, "Doctor, I would like to die. Can you help me?"

The doctor said, "No, and don't ask me again."

And I thought: I can write a play about this.

That's a mostly true story.

I've written maybe 20 plays, with more than 100 characters. Not a single character was based on a friend or relative. Not even close. That old adage "write about what you know" was wasted on me. My life experience fed my playwriting, of course, but the plays came more from research than from first-hand experience, and the characters were people I read about or imagined, not people I knew.

Getting to Room Temperature is a departure. It's a one-actor play and the actor plays "me." He tells my mother's story: we see photographs of her and hear her voice. She and my wife are named. Other characters, left unnamed, are nonetheless "real." This is a mostly true story: some things I forgot, some things I got wrong and didn't bother to fix*, some things are omitted to protect the guilty. A few things are made up.

I think my mother was an unusual and impressive woman, but I wouldn't have written a play about her had she not pursued euthanasia. And euthanasia — assisted dying, assisted suicide, all that — is an

---

* There's a story I remember from my Jewish upbringing: When truly religious people sew an article of clothing, they intentionally incorporate an imperfection where it doesn't show — out of humility, because God alone is perfect. In a similar spirit, if I discovered an inconsequential error, I sometimes left it in.

interesting and controversial subject, but I doubt I'd have written a play about it were my mother not an advocate. The two came together.

And I don't think I would have written about either were I not blessed or cursed with the ability or need to find humour in anything. How could you write about death, dying and euthanasia without humour? Who would possibly want to see such a play?

*   *   *

The response to *Getting to Room Temperature* has surprised me. Writing a play about my mother's dying sent me on a fascinating journey, and audiences have willingly come along. I found much of the experience surprisingly funny, and many in the audience seem to agree. And euthanasia is, of course, a current and controversial subject, and I thought my mother's story had something to tell us.

But often, what an audience gets out of a play is not what a playwright intentionally puts in. At a very basic level, *Getting to Room Temperature* is a story about a mother and son. It's been described as gentle, and even healing — and no one has ever accused me of that before.

Writing this play turned out to be a way for me to get to know my mother better; and producing it has kept my mother alive in an entirely pleasant way. This play is really a tribute to my mother, Rose Milner, and, as I say in the play, it would have been nice were she here to enjoy it.

ACKNOWLEDGEMENTS

Maureen Labonté and I were long-time colleagues, but I hadn't seen her for several years when we met in a Montreal café a few years ago. We talked mostly about our aging, ailing mothers and traded family stories. I told Maureen my mother had asked me to help her die, and Maureen encouraged me to write a play about it. I think I already was, but I'm not entirely sure.

I sent bits and pieces to Maureen, and eventually a draft. Maureen has, I think, an unerring sense of what works in theatre, and she is always willing to tell you when you've burst its bounds — when you've gone on at length on some political rant or otherwise abandoned your story for too long. And she knows that we make theatre for the public, not for our colleagues. Maureen, with others, urged me to include, God forbid, more of my own feelings. But I don't think she ever asked me a question when she knew the answer; and she never once had me arrested. I owe her a great deal.

Then Martin Conboy jumped on board; set and lighting designer and friend, we had worked together for years on a great many projects. Then Jenny Salisbury, a student of "community-engaged performance," said she could arrange workshop presentations at the University of Toronto, and did so much more. Next, Robert

Bockstael, wonderful actor and long-time friend, asked to read the script. "If you read it, you have to perform it," I said. And he did. And he committed himself beyond the calls of friendship and duty. Then we approached costume designer Sue Fijalkowska, with whom many of us had worked for years. Like everyone else, she leapt in. Everyone agreed to be paid when and if there was money. Everyone believed in this project.

So I thank them and I thank, too, Sabina Lysnes, my daughter, who watched this play about her grandmother and cried a great many times, and who edited this volume and cried some more. And Anne Hennessy, friend and geriatric psychiatrist (i.e., a psychiatrist who specializes in old people, *not* an old psychiatrist), who from the start believed in the importance of this play and did everything she could to promote it. Anne also gave me Sherwin B. Nuland's *How We Die: Reflections on Life's Final Chapter*, a book that changed my life and probably my death.

I thank also the following individuals who contributed in a great many ways: Danielle Alfaro, Darryl Bennett, Jon Carter, Eric Coates, Jean Marc Dalpé, Patrick Gauthier, Seth Gerry, Amelia Farrugia, Erin Kennedy, Tita Kyrtsakas, Sean Lamothe, Patrick McDonald, Henry Milner, Sarah Phillips, Cyd Rainville, Paul Rainville, Chris Ralph, Pat Thompson, Emma Tibaldo, Jessica Watkin, Alexandra Watt-Simpson. And these organizations: the Canada Council for the Arts; the Centre for Drama, Theatre and Performance Studies at the University of Toronto; the Great Canadian Theatre Company; Playwrights' Workshop Montréal; The Acting Company; and *undercurrents festival 2016*.

And finally, noted thespian Jennifer Brewin, artistic director of Common Boots Theatre and also my wife, who watched an early performance of *Getting to Room Temperature* and said (in a tone that indicated a bit too much surprise, if you ask me): "It's really good." This book is dedicated to Jennifer.

GETTING TO ROOM
TEMPERATURE

ROBERT BOCKSTAEL IN GETTING TO ROOM TEMPERATURE • PHOTO CREDIT: DEREK PRICE

Getting to Room Temperature premiered at the *undercurrents* festival, at the Arts Court Theatre in Ottawa, Canada, on February 10, 2016, produced by the Room Temperature Collective.

performed by	Robert Bockstael
director	Arthur Milner
dramaturge	Maureen Labonté
set and lighting design	Martin Conboy
costume design	Sue Fijalkowska
assistant director and producer	Jenny Salisbury
technical director	Ted Forbes
assistant stage manager	Kiersten MacDonald

A note on the production

According to its accompanying notes, Spalding Gray's *Swimming to Cambodia* (Dramatic Publishing Company) "was designed for one person to perform but the director has permission to make this into multiple roles if he/she so desires." Then the set is described, with the caveat that "each production is not obligated to do it this way." As for the regular sips of water that for Gray were "essential for the flow of the piece ... again, the director may use them anyway he/she deems appropriate and necessary."

The production notes below are offered in a similar spirit.

Getting to Room Temperature was written for one actor, a male in his 60s.

Set should be simple. We used a carpet, a stool and a small, high table on stage right. A projection screen was suspended stage left. The projections are of the writer's family and of paintings, people and animals mentioned. I've provided some of the projections in this publication; for the others, I've provided a URL (in the appendix).

Descriptions of the paintings, quotations from Margaret Somerville, etc., were "read" from file cards.

The section titles in the script indicate a shift, but are not to be spoken aloud.

References

All the quotations are edited for clarity and brevity. Those from Margaret Somerville are from a speech at the University of Tasmania in June 2011 (www.youtube.com/watch?v=SEdj6BRhMR0); articles in the National Post of October 27, 2014 (news.nationalpost.com/full-comment /margaret-somerville-rejecting-euthanasia-and-respecting-the-secular-spirit); and articles in the Prairie Messenger of November 12, 2014 (prairiemessenger.ca/14_11_12/dnews_14_11_12_1.html).

The information about nursing homes comes from the Canadian Institute for Health Information (https://secure.cihi.ca/free_products/CCRS_QualityinLongTermCare_EN.pdf).

The information on "the best countries in which to grow old" comes from the Halifax Chronicle Herald (thechronicleherald.ca/careincrisis/1168351-a-better-way-to-care-for-the-aging#.VRRWKlxN3zL).

I cite two books: *How We Die: Reflections on Life's Final Chapter* by Dr. Sherwin B. Nuland (Vintage 1995) and *Final Exit: The Practicalities of Self-Deliverance and Assisted Suicide for the Dying* by Derek Humphrey

(Random House 2002). I'm also indebted to *Being Mortal, Medicine and What Matters in the End* by Atul Gawande (Random House 2014) and *The World Until Yesterday: What Can We Learn from Traditional Societies?* by Jared Diamond (Viking 2012).

GETTING TO ROOM TEMPERATURE

1. PROLOGUE

(audio; lights up gradually as performer enters, listens)

"You have one saved message. Main menu. To revue — First saved message. Sent on July 20th at 4:28 PM, from 5-1-4-7-3 — Arthur, this is your mother. I can't tell you any news. I don't feel special good. I wish I would be better, but I hope. So be well. Give my regards to Jennifer. Wish her all the best. If she needs something, let her tell me. Bye, dear. Have a good day."

1

2. DAD FIRST

When I was eight years old, I would gather with my colleagues to contemplate the world. One story that intrigued us was about the old Eskimo who, when no longer able to contribute to his community, wandered off into the snowy night, never to be heard from again. And we wise eight-year-olds would shrug and say: "Well, that makes sense."

(projection 1 in: Rose)

My spry mother was ninety-three and a half when she took a turn for the worse. I accompanied her to the doctor. He closed a file on his desk, turned to her and said, "Rose, what can I do for you?"

My mother said, "Doctor, I would like to die. Can you help me?"

And I was reminded of that old Inuk, who didn't want to be a drain on his team.

This is a story about my mother.

(projection 1 out: Rose)

My *father* died 25 years ago.

He was in bed, at his home in Montreal. The end was in sight, but I thought I could make it back to Ottawa for a few days. So I was in his

3

bedroom to say goodbye. Well, to sit with him. He hadn't been able to talk for several days. His breathing was hard, raspy. He seemed in pain. I took his hand. There were some unusual choking sounds, and a spasm through his body, and then nothing.

He's dead, I thought. But I also thought: I better make sure. I don't want to go out into the hallway and announce, "he's dead," and then find out I was wrong. I felt his pulse. There was nothing, but I was so anxious that I didn't trust my perception. I was about to lift his eyelids, like they do on television, but I realized I had no idea what to look for. I got a small mirror from the bathroom, and held it to his mouth and nose. Nothing. Then I thought: that's another thing I've seen on television. Maybe it's just a television thing.

I held the mirror to my own mouth. Sure enough, it fogged up. But maybe my father was breathing very lightly. I tried again. Nothing. I got close to my father, my ear by his mouth. Nothing.

Someone pushed open the door: the palliative care nurse. "I think he's dead." She took out her stethoscope and put it to his heart.

My mother, my daughter, my brother and his wife were in the kitchen. I said, "Dad's dead." Everyone looked at the nurse. My mother screamed a short, sharp scream. The reactions were small. No one was surprised by this death.

My father was 70 when he found out he had cancer. He'd been healthy and robust and went to work every day. He had surgery and he had radiation and then more radiation.

After about a year, we knew he would not recover. Under the circumstances, it's important to keep one's sense of humour. After a particularly gloomy hospital visit, there was a dark silence between my brother and me. I asked him, "Did you hear about the guy who goes to see his doctor? Doctor says, 'Your tests came back. You have cancer and you have six months to live.' 'Wait a second,' says the guy, 'I want a second opinion.' 'Alright,' says the doctor, 'You're ugly, too.'"

My brother laughed. I continued. "Guy goes to see his doctor. Doctor says, 'I have bad news, and I have worse news.' Guy says, 'Let's start with the bad news.' Doctor says, 'You have cancer and you have 24 hours to live.' '24 hours to live? What could be worse than that?' Doctor says, 'I meant to call you yesterday.'"

We both laughed. "Guy goes to see a doctor. 'Your test results are in,' says the doctor, 'You have cancer. And you also have Alzheimer's.' 'Well,' says the guy, 'At least I don't have cancer.'"

My father never gave up and he never acknowledged to us that he was dying. I'm not sure he told himself. By the time it was obvious, he couldn't talk.

We sat Shiva — the seven days of mourning with time off for the Sabbath — and I hung around for a couple of days and then I said to my mother, "I'm going home. But if anything comes up, if you need me for anything, I'm two hours away. Don't hesitate. Just call." And my mother said, "Look, I'm not the first widow in the world and I won't be the last."

(projection 2 in: Ben and Rose)

When my father got sick, my mother was inconsolable. The doctor said he should drink a lot of water, my mother pushed water on him like it could cure cancer. It sometimes seemed she would die before him.

But now she said, "I'm not the first widow in the world and I won't be the last."

(projection 2 out: Ben and Rose)

3. LIVING ALONE

I had never seen, or perhaps noticed, that kind of stoicism in my mother. It's fair to say that my father's death was for her a watershed. She missed him, of course. Anniversaries were difficult. Family dinners were always touched by sadness.

She had been a housewife, a homemaker or, as we used to say, "She didn't work." At 70, she didn't go out and get a job, but she became tougher, more confident, more resolute.

More opinionated, too — not always a good thing. She decided she supported the death penalty: "When there are many witnesses and they are caught in the act, they should be put to death." My parents had always voted Liberal, but my mother decided she liked Stephen Harper: "He's a very nice man and he's a good friend of Israel." She decided she supported euthanasia: "If a person is miserable and makes everyone else miserable, why should she live? When my time comes, you won't have to beg me."

She also didn't like children. She said she did, and I'm sure she believed she loved her great-grandchildren. She insisted they visit regularly and then she yelled at them.

She was convinced she didn't have a hearing problem. I'd say, "The television is so loud the walls are shaking." She'd say, "It doesn't sound loud to me." She'd constantly ask people to repeat themselves. I thought it important she get a hearing aid and tried to enlist the help of others. She'd ask, "Do I have a problem hearing?" My brother and nephew would stare sheepishly like it was the first they'd heard of it. My own wife would say to me: "Well, you do mumble."

These were details. In her 70s and 80s, she was more active and more fun than she'd ever been.

For twenty years she lived alone, in the big family house. My father had made sure she wanted for nothing money could buy. My nephew helped her with various domestic chores.

My brother and I visited, sometimes with wives and children and grandchildren.

But mostly she passed her time talking on the phone to or visiting friends. She went to Florida for the winter because, she said, all her friends went. She was slowing down, but at 85 she could still go for an hour-long walk.

My parents had had a large circle of friends. My father was among the first to die. He started a trend. Soon, more and more were dead, dying or demented. Increasingly, my mother's social activities involved visits to hospitals and cemeteries. Eventually she was down to friends of friends, and then friends of friends of friends.

I talked to her several times about moving into a residence. I encouraged her to visit a few, so that she'd know where she wanted to go. But she refused. "I'm not one of those people who won't move. When the time comes for me to move, I will know."

One day, my nephew said to my brother and me: "We have to do something. She calls me every day. I don't mind helping her, but I can't be her only friend."

I came from Ottawa for a special family meeting. I said, "You should move into a seniors' residence, where there would be a lot of people and a lot of things to do." My brother said, "Stay in your nice home and we'll find someone to move in with you." She said, "I'll think about it." My nephew said, "You can think about it, but two months from now you're either in a residence or someone's moving in."

Word came quickly. She picked a residence where she had a friend. We went to look at her friend's apartment. My mother admitted it was very nice. We spoke with the activities coordinator. There were indeed a lot of activities. I said, "I'd live here!" My mother laughed. This was going well.

We met with the executive director. He explained that meals were optional. Breakfast, he said, was at eight o'clock. "That's very early," said my mother. "You don't have to go," said my brother. "You could eat in your apartment." My mother said: "I'm going for breakfast. Why would I want to eat alone?"

4. LIVING WITH OTHERS

(projection 3 in: Retirement Home)

From the moment she moved in, she demonstrated her ability to adapt to the inevitable: she treated the move like it had been her idea from the start. And she made the best of it: she played cards, she watched the Monday and Thursday movies, she attended afternoon concerts. She built little boxes out of popsicle sticks.

In comparison with her housemates, my mother was agile. If they held a race for everyone, she would win. There were a great many people with walkers, so the competition wasn't stiff.

(projection 3 out: Retirement Home)

My mother didn't mind the people in walkers. She wasn't in a hurry. It drove me crazy. Getting in and out of elevators was excruciating. I felt trapped behind this slow-motion herd. I had fantasies about pushing them into a heap of skinny legs and aluminum tubing.

My mother did have two complaints. The food — "I tell the cooks: use a little garlic" — and people with dementia who gathered in the sitting area in front of the elevators. My mother avoided them like the plague. One day, a woman approached her. She appeared healthy and younger than the others. "Rose, don't you know me?"

"Yes, of course, Rachel. How are you?"

"I'm Rachel."

"I know. It's nice to see you."

"I'm Rachel. Don't you remember me?"

"Yes, Rachel, I do."

"Don't you know me?"

My mother walked away.

"Do you know her?"

My mother turned to me. "You remember Mrs. Weinberg? They were good friends. This is why I didn't need to visit a home. You think I was never in a residence for old people? I didn't need to see this."

5. FLORIDA

My family arrived in Montreal in 1951.

My parents had narrowly escaped the Holocaust. When the Germans entered Poland, my parents and some friends went to Russia, expecting either to return home or to be joined by their families. Neither happened.

They survived the war in Uzbekistan, working in a textile factory.

When the war was over, they headed west, to Europe, to search for relatives — without success. They ended up in a displaced persons camp in the American sector of Germany.

(projection 4 in: Family Portrait)

Six years later, we were accepted for immigration to Canada. My brother was five, I was one.

Some people who endured those times dwelt on them all their lives. Others did their best to put it behind them. I am grateful that my parents were among the latter.

(projection 4 out: Family Portrait)

My father had been a Zionist from an early age. Like a good teenager, I enjoyed picking fights with my parents, and Israel was the perfect subject. Our biggest fights were about Israel. But I matured and did my best to avoid the subject with my mother.

One evening — she was 91, I think — I was visiting her in Florida, we were watching the television news. There was an item about Israel. My mother said, "Israel wants peace." I pretended I hadn't heard.

She tried again. "All they want is peace." I closed my ears.

"I know Israel," she said. "They just want peace." I took the bait.

"Look, you like President Obama."

"He's a very good man."

"For two years he's been asking Israel to stop building settlements. But Israel refuses. Why?"

"Israel wants peace."

"He begs them to stop building, but they refuse. Why?"

"They just want peace."

The next evening we went out for dinner with my mother's friends. We were all mocking Egypt's President Mubarak, who was then weeks away from resignation. Someone pointed out he had 75 billion dollars in the bank.

I said: "The Americans gave him 2 billion a year for 30 years. Where did he get the rest?"

"Interest," said Mr. Stern. Everyone laughed.

I said, "The Americans give Israel 3 billion a year."

"Ah. The money for Mubarak is a bribe. The money for Israel is like a gift to a close friend."

There was a brief silence. My mother spoke: "Why does Israel keep building settlements?"

I was stunned. As was Mr. Stern. "Why shouldn't they? It's their country. Everyone can build in his own country."

I said: "No one thinks the West Bank belongs to Israel."

Mr. Stern leaned in: "Israel has many enemies."

"Yes, but even the United States — Israel's "good friend" — says the West Bank doesn't belong to Israel."

There was a silence. Again my mother spoke: "So why does Israel keep building settlements?"

Mr. Stern mumbled: "We should order desert." But I didn't care. For the first time in my life, my mother actually listened to something I said. For the first time ever, we were political allies. I could see us on a speaking tour across the country — or maybe a two-person play: "Mother and Son: Conflict and Reconciliation." This was something new. We were a team. Either that or it was the first sign of dementia.

The next day I reminded my mother of our conversation with her friends. "Don't bother me with settlements. Israel just wants peace."

The dementia had passed.

6. THE FALL

I would visit my mother at the residence maybe once a month. We would go for half-hour walks, outdoors in good weather, in malls in bad. We'd go out to eat and to movies. She couldn't hear — she'd fall asleep and then she'd say, "They don't make good movies anymore."

She liked it when my wife came with me. She told Jennifer, "Nature has been good to you, but you can always improve on nature." My mother put eye shadow on her, a bit of rouge. They laughed.

My mother had been in the residence for two years. It was definitely better than living alone, and she never expressed regret. My sister-in-law suggested she was deteriorating faster than she would have at home, because here almost everything was done for her. It might be true. I think her increasing deafness was a factor in her deterioration, because, well, "hear nothing, learn nothing." But at ninety-three and a half, she was, as we say, spry. She was active. She laughed.

Once a week, she would walk to the local library to get books with big letters. One day at the library, she tripped. She didn't break anything but she had some pain and then it went away. One morning, about a month later, I got a call telling me my mother was in the hospital. She'd been short of breath, and the nurse at the residence called an ambulance. My brother and nephew were out of town, and by the time I heard about it she'd been in the hospital for two days. She was still in the emergency ward. It could have been a movie about a third-world country — one cot against another, constant noise, impossible to get anyone's attention.

A nice young doctor told me a lung infection had been treated but he'd kept her there because she seemed to be suffering from "mild dementia." By way of example, he asked if she knew who I was. "My son, Arthur."

"Where do you live?"

"Here."

"Where are we?"

"We're at home, in my—" *(then uncertain)* "Aren't we?"

It was pathetic. Clearly, she was disoriented, but was she here because she was disoriented or was she disoriented because she was here?

"Where do you live, mom? What city?"

"Montreal."

"Where do I live?"

"Ottawa."

"I'm taking her home."

"Good," said the doctor, "I've written a new prescription. I think one of the drugs she was taking might have led to the lung problem."

An hour later, we were back at the residence. Some of the staff helped her into bed.

A few days later, rested and comfortable, her "mild dementia" was gone. But the truth is, everything had changed. She was sleepy, she lost her appetite, she was unsteady on her feet. She decided to use a walker, she said, "Just until I get my strength back."

I don't remember when it was, exactly, that she first said that she wanted to die.

7. DYING

She told me and she told my brother and my nephew. And on the phone she told her granddaughter, my daughter. She wanted to go to Switzerland, where she'd heard they practice euthanasia.

None of us was outraged. We considered her request legitimate. On the other hand, we weren't eager to help.

My daughter and nephew were happy to leave the matter to my brother and me. We did not act rashly.

I found out that Switzerland is the only country that will help foreigners kill themselves. But it's a long process. You can't just show up at the airport and get a shot in the arm.

I told my mother it would take time to make arrangements. Meanwhile, I said, you'll probably get better. That seemed to satisfy her. We let it go. Really, I did nothing.

Looking back, it didn't seem a big thing. I'm sure it was for her. And it should have been for me. Being asked to help your mother kill herself is — what? Unexpected? Unnatural? It made me uncomfortable, and I brushed it aside. And for a few weeks, it didn't come up.

We went to see her doctor. He closed a file on his desk, turned to her and said, "Rose, what can I do for you?"

My mother said, "Doctor, I would like to die. Can you help me?"

The doctor said, "No, and don't ask me again."

We told him about the stay in the hospital, about the shortness of breath, about the disorientation. We showed him the new prescription. He said, "I don't see why they changed her medication. It wasn't what caused her breathing problem and it might be what's making her dizzy."

"I'm very tired," said my mother.

"Well," said the doctor, "you're not a young woman." Which was news to us.

8. TWO STEPS BACK

Soon she was unable to take more than a few steps on her own. We stopped going to movies and then restaurants. It was too much effort, and she didn't want to be seen with her walker.

The main thing was loss of energy. On bad days, she'd fall asleep constantly. And when she was half asleep, she'd lose all sense of where she was. One evening she spoke to me in Polish for five minutes. Which was fascinating because I don't speak Polish. There were also good days, when she was sharp and wanted to go for a walk in the mall across the road.

It occurred to me at the time that doctors could tell the difference between someone who is sick from a disease and someone who's sick from old age. If you're sick from a disease, they try to cure it, even if it's cancer. But if you're sick from old age, well, it's not urgent.

One indication that you've crossed the threshold from sick to old is that doctors will change your prescription at the drop of a hat. My brother suggests to her *new* doctor that she's depressed, and the doctor says, "I'll put her on anti-depressants." My daughter suggests the anti-depressants are making my mother tired, and the doctor says, "We'll cut back." It's a lottery. She's on six different drugs. One pill makes you sleepy, but maybe it's keeping you alive. And you mix it with five more pills, who knows what it's doing? The residence had a doctor who visited one afternoon a week. And he's supposed to keep track of 120 old people on six different prescriptions each. The truth is, in terms of serious care of the elderly, it's amateur hour.

My brother and his wife believed Rose was depressed. They thought she was less depressed after she was put on anti-depressants, but some of us disagreed. It was hard to tell. My brother said she didn't talk about dying as much and was generally more positive. But she always went in spurts.

I thought: I don't want to treat her search for death as a sign of illness. There's a circular logic: "She wants to die, but it's because she's depressed." "How do you know she's depressed?" "Because she wants to die." There's something unfair about that. I preferred to take her at her word.

I came to visit her one time, and she was asleep in the nice back yard the residence. I was sitting beside her, reading, when she woke up. She said, "Why did you come?" "To see you." "Why? You have better things to do."

We use a lot of euphemisms. It seems the more anxious we are about something, the more expressions we have for it.

Vomit. Regurgitate, throw up, barf, puke, talk to Ralph on the big white telephone.

Sex.

Dead. Deceased, late, passed, passed away, departed, gone, kicked the bucket, kicked the can, bought the farm, bit the dust, sleeping with the fishes, at room temperature, singing with the choir invisible, pushing up daisies, in a better place.

I don't think my mother was depressed. She was matter of fact. Her life was no fun, and she knew it was all downhill from there. She had reached a decision. She wanted *to die*, and she didn't understand why no one would help her. She was beyond euphemisms. But the rest of us were embarrassed.

9. THE SUICIDE KIT

So I started to take it seriously.

First, I asked myself: Am I capable of this?

I reviewed my murderous past.

A long time ago, on a farm, I killed a chicken with an axe.

I've caught many fish with hooks and bashed their heads in with sticks.

I came across a kitten, once, that was half run over and flopping on the highway. I backed up, aimed carefully, and crushed its skull.

A few years ago, in the country, a friend asked for my help. She had found a small falcon. It couldn't stand. You could see it had a broken neck. She said, "I think one of the dogs did it. I think we should kill it, but no one will. Jennifer said you'd kill it. Jennifer says you do that kind of thing." Thank you, Jennifer.

I'm not suggesting that killing a human being is like killing a non-human animal. But I point out that the chicken, fish, kitten and falcon were not asking to be killed. My mother, however, was.

Well, why ask me? Why ask your son? Why not a stranger ... like the doctor? Why not go march across an ice floe, with that Eskimo?

And wait a second. Is that story even true? Cause if it isn't — I thought — I'm off the hook.

Well, it turns out that the intentional death of old people is pretty common among nomads, who found it hard to take old people with them, and also in environments with severe food shortages, like the far north. The dying might happen through simple abandonment, or in the old person wandering off, or by actual killing.

Here's an example. Among the Kaulong people of New Guinea, "the strangling of a widow by her brother or son immediately after her husband's death was routine until the 1950s." And it was demanded by the widow. One reluctant son described how his mother humiliated him: "My mother spoke loudly so all could hear: 'My son won't kill me because he wants to have sex with me.'"

I did not share this bit of research with my mother.

Here's another thought. Maybe my mother wasn't serious.

"Alright, mom. Here I have a syringe filled with something. Do you want to die? Yes or no?"

Filled with what? I searched the Web.

I typed in "suicide kit" and found a story about an 86-year-old woman in California who had been arrested for selling helium suicide kits for $14.95, which struck me as quite a good price, even with the strong U.S. dollar.

The theory is this: If you put a bag over your head to cut off oxygen, you will provoke a choking reflex, which is extremely painful, and you will struggle to rip the bag off your head. But by substituting an inert gas, you ... just ... drift ... away. Apparently it takes about two minutes to lose consciousness and you're dead in five.

(projection 5 in: Suicide Kit)

Here's what the kit looks like. Helium is the easiest inert gas to get, at a party store, for blowing up balloons, and you'll be talking like Donald Duck as you say goodbye, which makes the whole thing even more fun.

Next. You can get a few feet of three-eighths-inch-diameter plastic tubing at any hardware store.

And you'll need a plastic bag about the size of a pillowcase. Don't use a pillowcase. Clear plastic is best, so you can see what's happening.

Attach the tube to the plastic bag with masking or electrical tape. Put the bag over your head and seal it around your neck with tape or a colourful ribbon. It doesn't have to be very tight.

(projection 5 out: Suicide Kit)

Now the thing is, and this is maybe the key point: this is a suicide kit. I wasn't contemplating suicide. I was contemplating, well, murder. And the thing about murder is, you don't want to get caught.

So. I would help my mother with the kit, and when she falls asleep I leave. I try to sneak out unseen and — No. I walk past the front desk, waving goodbye, just like somebody who hasn't killed his mother. Then, when they find her, I act surprised and cry. — That's not going to work. They'd figure out she didn't buy the kit on her own, and I'd be suspect number one.

So. I have to take everything with me. The question is: would an autopsy find traces of helium? It's inert, so it would — stay helium. But it's a gas, so it would float away. And, can I get in and out without being seen? Carrying a big orange tank.

Well there goes that. I will call the police and loudly and proudly proclaim justifiable matricide. — And spend months and maybe years in jail, or at least fighting in court.

Maybe it was time to give helium a rest and consider the alternatives. I went to Chapters. I must say that their euthanasia section is disappointing. They had one book:

(projection 6 in: Final Exit)

"Final Exit: The Practicalities of Self-Deliverance and Assisted Suicide for the Dying" by Derek Humphrey. "The Number One New York Times Bestseller."

I read the table of contents as I was standing in line to pay. Chapter 3 was "Beware of the Law." Chapter 19: "How Do You Get the "Magic Pills"? "Magic Pills" was in quotation marks.

(projection 6 out: Final Exit)

I hand the clerk a credit card. He puts the receipt in the book, like they do, and I walk out and — break into a cold sweat. There on the receipt is my name, the title of the book, and the date. It will forever say somewhere in the Chapters computer cloud that, on the 17th of May, I bought "Final Exit." So this is my first complaint about this book: It should say, in great big letters on the cover, "Pay cash."

You'd think someone who's watched four thousand episodes of *Law & Order* would be better prepared.

Well that simplified things. "Magic pills" or not, I was not going to get away with murder. So I avoided the question. I went back to letting my mother suffer. Anyway, it was time for me to face the awful truth. I did not want to kill my mother. I'm selfish. I'm a bad son.

10. MARGARET SOMERVILLE

Or maybe not.

At the age of eight, I had considered suicide by elderly Inuit reasonable. Maybe it was time to reconsider. Maybe there exist strong ethical and philosophical arguments against suicide and assisted suicide. Maybe there is reason to say to my mother: "I'm sorry, but what you're asking is wrong."

I wish I could say that as I researched the arguments against euthanasia I underwent a great internal struggle. To assist or not to assist. To kill or not to kill. To be or not to be. I wish I could say that I was deeply moved by Rick Santorum's ravings or Margaret Somerville's measured argument, that they stirred within me great misgivings on the morality of hastening death by even one millisecond.

But I think it's this. There are two kinds of people in the world. There are people like me who, when I was eight years old, heard about the old Eskimo and said, "Why not?" And then there are people who are just outraged.

That's it. There's not a lot of "undecided" and there's not a lot of "no opinion."

And if you're one of the outraged, well, no one is going to convince you that your outrage is misplaced. And all your arguments — well, let me list them, even though they're not going to convince people like me.

(projection 7 in: Margaret Somerville)

These are from articles and speeches by Margaret Somerville, founding director of McGill University's Centre for Medicine, Ethics and Law, and Canada's leading opponent of assisted dying.

(projection 7 out: Margaret Somerville)

One. *(reads)* "Once you legalize euthanasia, you cannot stop the expansion of justifications for it." This is the famous "slippery slope" argument. We'll start by killing only those who are in pain, have terminal illnesses and ask to be killed, and pretty soon we'll be killing the disabled, the inconvenient — and the very annoying *(points, at random)* like you in the blue shirt.

Two. *(reads)* "Kill the pain, not the person with the pain." According to this view, we don't need euthanasia, we need more palliative care and better painkillers.

Three. *(reads)* "One of the main reasons old people want to die is they're worried about being a burden on their family." In other words, it's not really about pain.

I want to intervene here, because it threw me a bit. Is it true? I'm pretty sure my mother believed she was a burden on her family. She definitely knew she was no fun to hang out with. And I'm sure it occurred to her more than once that she was using up her children and grandchildren and great-grandchildren's inheritance. And the care she was getting from the medical system in the last stages of her life — did she think about government healthcare expenses? I don't know. But should people worry about that?

Four. *(reads)* "I believe accepting euthanasia will seriously damage our sense of amazement, wonder and awe at both who we are and the universe we inhabit ... Euthanasia treats us as expired products to be checked out of the supermarket of life." That's pretty good.

Five. *(reads)* "It's very difficult in a secular society to respond to the relief of suffering argument. ... In the kind of secular societies we are, it's extraordinarily hard to give any meaning or value to suffering."

I was going to let that go, but I can't help myself. I want Margaret Somerville to tell my ailing, 94-year-old mother, who lost her entire family to the Nazis, that a little more suffering is exactly what she needs.

Six. *(reads)* "What has happened that has made us think that euthanasia is a good idea? I think the reasons are societal-level reasons. We've had a breakdown of families." People "feel unloved and alone. ... Part of that is to do with the different structure of families that we have today. You see those old paintings, somebody lying on a bed with everybody around them, holding their hand and the guy with the white nightcap on and his white nightgown and it all looks rather sort of peaceful."

That's nice. It's nice.

11. A COMFORTABLE DEATH

I couldn't find that particular painting. I did find these.

(projection 8 in; then multiple crossfades until projection 17)

The dying man is Leonardo da Vinci. That is not Leonardo's loving son consoling him, but rather Francis I, King of France.

This is "The Death of Hervor." She's a character from a 13th century saga and was "a renowned shieldmaiden who dressed like a man, fought, killed and pillaged under her male surname Hjörvard."

"The Administration of the Eucharist to a Dying Person."

"Cardinal Mazarin Dying." Jules Mazarin was an Italian cardinal, diplomat and politician, and chief minister of France from 1642 until his death in 1661.

"The Death of General Wolfe." James Wolfe led the British to victory at the Battle of the Plains of Abraham in 1759.

"St. Barbara Comforting a Dying Man with the Last Sacrament."

"Cleopatra and Mark Antony Dying." Defeated by Octavian's forces at the Battle of Actium in 31 BC, the lovers fled to Egypt, where they committed suicide.

"The Doctor."

"A child dying of tuberculosis, a common ailment in the 1800s."
"Jesus Dying on the Cross."

(projection 17 out)

It's nice to be surrounded by people as you die, but it helps to be the king's friend or a general or God.

Note that, in these paintings, selected pretty much at random, the about-to-be-deceased are not very old: Two children under the age of ten. Wolfe was 32. Jesus is said to have been 33. Mazarin at 59 and Da Vinci at 67 were the oldest.

12. SAYING GOODBYE

My mother was 94 when she died.

My father was 72.

(projection 18 in: Ben)

He was president of a synagogue for 30 years. He believed that religion was necessary to the survival of the Jewish people, but when I asked him if he believed in God, he would say, "People need something to believe in." He observed some of the traditional rules — at home, his diet was traditionally kosher, which is to say not kosher. Away from home, in restaurants, he would eat seafood and even pork, though only when carefully camouflaged in Chinese food.

And then my father got cancer. He had chemotherapy and when the cancer came back he had radiation. I remember thinking at the time that when you were diagnosed with cancer you had a certain survival rate, depending on the type of cancer. If the cancer returned after treatment, your odds of survival went way down. And if, after the second treatment, the cancer came back again, well, that was it. His doctors seemed to agree. They pretty much gave up.

My father didn't give up. He paid a lot of money to a top Rabbi in New York City to pray for him and get him an appointment with a top doctor. And he paid a lot of money to see that doctor.

I went with him. The doctor said, "We have every reason to be optimistic. I can put together a protocol that has been very successful at treating cancers such as yours."

The New York doctor sent the "cure" to the Montreal doctor. The Montreal doctor said, "This is very similar to the combination of drugs you've had. And it will be difficult for you. You're not as strong as you were a year ago."

But my father insisted. He was supposed to get two treatments. The first treatment almost killed him. He never got the second one.

If you pay a Rabbi and a doctor a lot of money, you might not get cured, but you will get optimism.

(projection 18 out: Ben)

When my mother got sick, she never turned to miracle cures. She never turned to religion. She didn't ask to see the Rabbi or his wife, with whom she was close.

Of course, my father was 72 when he died. My mother was 94.

My father got sick before he got old; and my mother got old before she got sick.

Here's what Margaret Somerville gets wrong. She thinks we're in danger of going from a world in which God decides when we die, to one in which strangers decide.

But in fact we're long past God deciding. Science and society have extended our lives, not God. If Somerville wants God to decide, we'll have to get rid of not just the vaccines and penicillin, but — let's admit it — the unions and public health care and the welfare state. And we'll have to go back to dying at 40 instead of 80. It is now, for the most part, doctors, under a set of guidelines and laws created by politicians and bureaucrats, who decide when and how we die.

I think people like me want to take the decision away from doctors and bureaucrats, but we don't want to give it back to God. We're grateful for the modern conveniences, but we want to make the decision ourselves.

13. A FEW TIPS

My mother decided to move into a retirement home. At the time, I thought a retirement home and a nursing home were the same thing.

A retirement home, also known as a seniors' residence, is like living in an apartment building. My mother had her own unit, came and left as she pleased, but she ate breakfast and dinner in a dining room, and if she didn't show up for a meal, someone came to look for her.

If you don't have enough money, or your family can't or won't look after you, and you can't look after yourself, you will end up in a nursing home, also known as a long-term care facility. You sign over your old-age pension cheque, and they will take care of you. You'll be in a shared room or a dormitory with no privacy. You'll be told when and which drugs to take, when the lights go on, when they go off.

According to the Canadian Institute for Health Information, *(reads)* "The average nursing home resident in Canada is 85 or older and faces many challenges, including multiple chronic diseases and problems with mobility, memory and incontinence."

"60 per cent suffer from dementia, including Alzheimer's disease."

According to researchers, Denmark, Sweden and the Netherlands are the best countries in which to grow old. Of course, their citizens pay the highest taxes in the world.

So here's some advice about growing old in Canada: Don't be poor.

14. HOW WE DIE

(projection 19 in: Nuland)

In *How We Die: Reflections on Life's Final Chapter*, Dr. Sherwin B. Nuland says movies and TV shows get it wrong. They create a false impression. In real life, dying old people scream, they have raw bedsores over half their bodies, they retch and gasp for air, they defecate on themselves or fall out of bed or onto the bathroom floor. On television and in the movies, they slip quietly, sadly, politely way.

Nuland describes the autopsies of people who died at 85 and older. Their death certificates had reported cause of death as heart attack, stroke, cancer or infection — those were the big ones — but in every case the autopsy found that they were dying of other things at the same time.

(projection 19 out: Nuland)

In other words, maybe they died of an infection but they were this far from having a stroke. In other words, their whole system was collapsing. In other words, they were at the end of their *life span*.

(projection 20 in: Tortoise)

A Galapagos land tortoise lives to 190.

(crossfade to projection 21: Squirrel)

A very healthy grey squirrel barely makes it to 20.

(projection 21 out: Squirrel)

Those are life spans. The human life span is about 90, and that hasn't changed for thousands of years. What has changed, for humans, is life expectancy. In 1900, Canadians could expect to live to 50. Now we expect to live into our 80s.

My mother's age, 94, used to be a rare achievement. Now it's par for the course. This is a key point: for the first time in the history of the world, human life expectancy in the rich countries is very close to the human life span.

That means we die differently. In 1900, your typical person got sick — at 17 or 57 — and died at home a few days later. Today, most of us die in a hospital. And we don't get sick — we just get old, and then we linger. Pneumonia used to be called "the friend of the aged." Now it's easily cured. So we linger.

Of course, the longer people live, the higher the percentage of old people. We blame it on the baby boom, but if post-World War II babies like me died at 50, there would be no boom in old people now. Given the unprecedented millions of us who will be lingering for months or years, the current interest in euthanasia is not surprising.

The irony is that virtually none of the current discussion is about the aged. Quebec's legislation requires that candidates for assisted death "must suffer from an incurable serious illness" and "from constant and unbearable physical or psychological pain." The Supreme Court decision is pretty much the same.

These are humane and important steps, but they would likely have been of no use to my mother, and they won't much help the vast majority of people who in the years to come will suffer lingering deterioration. If we're going to talk about euthanasia, we need to distinguish between the young and the old, between people who get sick before they get old and people who get old before they get sick.

Let me make it crass. If you have a six-year-old car, and it's running well, and it needs a complete break job, get the break job. But if the car is 15 years old, and has 383 thousand kilometres on it, and the body's rusted and the motor's coughing black smoke, save your money.

If you're in your eighties or nineties and by some miracle your cancer is stopped ... well — If you stop breathing and the emergency team pounds your chest and breaks a few ribs and gets you breathing again — so what? You get to hang around in bed, unconscious, delusional or in pain, for a few more days or weeks.

All this my mother knew. In her body. In her brain. She knew she had turned the corner. I suspect each of us will know when we've turned the corner.

I'm not suggesting that your sons and daughters, or a committee at city hall, be empowered to measure your vital signs and dispatch you at an appropriate time.

I'm talking about myself. I'm trying to figure it out. I'm having a conversation with myself and I'm inviting you to listen in. I'm telling myself: Don't hang on for dear life. Don't consume your last penny and more. Don't fear death.

All this my mother knew. In her body. In her brain.

15. HOW ROSE DIED

(projection 22 in: Rose in July)

It's the middle of July. I'm visiting my mother. I help her into a wheelchair and we go for a walk in the bright sun. She has lunch in the dining hall and then she goes to arts and crafts. She's painting a small wooden box, but she keeps falling asleep.

(projection 22 out: Rose in July)

I go home to Ottawa and two days later she leaves a phone message.

(audio)

*"You have one saved message. Main menu. To review —
First saved message. Sent on July 20th at 4:28 PM, from
5-1-4-7-3 — Arthur, this is your mother. I can't tell you
any news. I don't feel especially good. I wish I would be
better, but I hope. So be well. Give my regards to Jennifer.
Wish her all the best. If she needs something, let her tell
me. Bye, dear. Have a good day."*

A few days after that, the breathing problems return and my brother takes her to emergency. The doctor wants to admit her, but my mother says no and she insists. The doctor and the nurses pressure her, and she looks at my brother. He says: "We'll do whatever you want." My brother takes her home. She gets into bed.

My brother calls me. He says that I should come, that she could die at any moment. Then he calls back: "Well, maybe not; it could be weeks, or months. We should stick to the original plan."

Which was this: My brother would stay with her for three days. Then I would come for a week while he and his wife went on vacation.

I call my brother every day. My mother doesn't get out of bed. She barely speaks or eats. I am thinking: She hates every minute of this. I cannot let her suffer week after week. When I get there, we'll talk about what she wants me to do.

Then my sister-in-law calls. Rose died, by herself, that afternoon.

So I got off easy. Rose left. She slipped away while no one was looking. I'm kind of proud of her.

My mother was a social pioneer. According to surveys, 84 per cent of us now support assisted dying. But twenty-five years ago, watching as her friends aged and died, my mother would say, "If a person is miserable and makes everyone else miserable, why should she live? When my time comes, you won't have to beg me."

She was right. She had to beg us.

16. IT'S MY PARTY

The truth is, I don't feel that bad about not helping her die. As deaths go, hers was okay. Ninety-four years old. Seven months of gradual decline. No excruciating pain, so far as I know. She never went into a nursing home.

What I do feel bad about is this: I should have organized a going-away party. A farewell party. She could have died at that gathering, surrounded by friends and the people who loved her.

I don't know how she would have felt about that. I don't know how many of the people close to her would have come. My wife said she wouldn't, it would be too macabre and too sad. Then she thought about it and said she would. I don't think death, a good death, which is a timely death, needs to be gruesome or even sad. I think the more we think about it and talk about it, the more natural and ordinary it becomes.

And so we all would have gathered in her home, and had some wine. She liked sweet drinks, so she might have had a liqueur. And I would have helped her with the plastic bag and the helium — or what would have been more elegant — if we could have found some — would be barbiturates. And we would have toasted her and held her hand and cried as she slipped away.

I think for me, that's what I would like. When I think I'm done, I will invite some people, we'll get good and drunk, and if I'm up for it I'll tell long, boring stories, and we'll laugh and cry and say goodbye.

My father's last weeks were in palliative care — no one was trying to save his life anymore. The nurses were great and, when we left a message, his palliative care doctor always got back to us within 10 minutes. We had decided he would die at home, but the doctor warned us that the tough part would be when he stopped eating: We'd want to send him to the hospital. And he warned us that my mother would be the weak link. And he was right. But we just told her: Mom, we all agreed we wanted him to die at home, and that's what's happening. And she accepted it.

So, I'll need to have the forethought to not die in a hospital. And I will need a friend brave enough to help me die, and I hope the laws will have changed so that no one goes to jail for killing someone ready and wanting to go.

The hardest part, of course, would be dementia, particularly Alzheimer's disease, which can leave our bodies healthy when our minds are gone. I would like to be able to sign a document today which stipulates that when, for a period of 30 days, I cannot recognize my grandchildren or remember their names, I will be put to death. But no country will allow me to sign a request today, when I am — arguably — of sound mind, for euthanasia to be carried out at a later date when I am not.

(projection 23 in: Rose b/w)

As for my mother, well, this is her party. It's not bad, lots of people. It would be better if there were family, of course, and if Rose were here, among us, to say goodbye.

Thank you.

(projection 23 out: Rose b/w)

(The end.)

APPENDIX

There are 23 projections, most in colour, some in black and white. Seven are included in this text: six photos of members of the playwright's family; and "Suicide Kit." Digital versions are available to producers.

Other images can be found on the Web. I've provided URLs, but there is no guarantee that they will remain operational. Most can be found by doing a simple search. Google's Advanced Image Search (<http://www.google.com/advanced_image_search>) is a useful tool for finding images in the public domain.

List of Projections

1. Rose (family collection)
2. Ben and Rose (family collection)
3. Retirement Home (photo of seniors on a park bench) <http://www.familysecuritymatters.org/imgLib/20120913_senior_citizens_park_bench_LARGE.jpg>
4. Family Portrait (family collection)
5. Suicide Kit (photo credit: Arthur Milner)

6. Final Exit (book cover) <http://t2.gstatic.com/images?q=t bn:ANd9GcSsbWrMgKnjaoZWAtIN1wF_e8biQad TMT1tzLPykrfc8j9aiQ1P>

7. Margaret Somerville <http://2.bp.blogspot.com/-7_eOUTgg LGU/UwuewckuJ-I/AAAAAAAAQg0/twHQ2lNZIEk/ s1600/Margaret+Somerville3.jpg>

8. Francis I at the Dying of Leonardo da Vinci. Louis Gallait, Belgian 1810-1887 <http://spinnet.eu/wiki-paintings/index. php/Francis_I_at_dying_da_Vinci>

9. Hervor's Death. Peter Nicolai Arbo, Norwegian 1831-1892 <http://en.wikipedia.org/wiki/Hervor>

10. Administration of the Eucharist to a Dying Person. Alexey Venetsianov, Russian 1780-1847 <https://en.wikipedia.org/ wiki/Viaticum#/media/File:Alexey_Venetsianov_25.jpg>

11. Cardinal Mazarin Dying. Paul Delaroche, French 1797-1856 <https://commons.wikimedia.org/wiki/File:Cardinal_ Mazarin_Dying.jpg>

12. The Death of General Wolfe. Benjamin West, Anglo-American 1728-1830 <http://en.wikipedia.org/wiki/ The_Death_of_General_Wolfe>

13. St. Barbara Comforting a Dying Man with the Last Sacrament. Joos Van Cleve, German/Belgian 1485-1541 <http://www. wikigallery.org/paintings/290001-290500/290199/painting1. jpg>

14. Cleopatra and Mark Antony Dying. Pompeo Batoni, Italian 1708-1787 <http://www.markantony.org/photo-gallery/cleopatra-and-mark-antony-dying-by-pompeo-batoni/>

15. The Doctor. Sir Luke Fildes, English 1843-1927 <http://www.tate.org.uk/art/artworks/fildes-the-doctor-n01522>

16. A Child Dying of Tuberculosis, a Common Ailment in the 1800s. No further information. <http://www.bbc.com/news/uk-25259505>

17. Jesus Dying on the Cross. No further information. <https://www.catholicculture.org/culture/liturgicalyear/pictures/stat12.jpg>

18. Ben (family collection)

19. Nuland (photo of author and book cover) <http://peacebenwilliams.com/wp-content/uploads/2014/03/NULAND.png>

20. Tortoise <http://blogs.sandiegozoo.org/wp-content/uploads/2014/09/6385762041_d8668db02a_z.jpg>

21. Squirrel. David Ruppert <http://www.pbase.com/dr24/image/60807049>

22. Rose in July (family collection)

23. Rose b/w (family collection)

ABOUT THE AUTHOR

Arthur Milner is a Canadian playwright, theatre director and journalist. Published plays include *Learning to Live with Personal Growth, 1997, Zero Hour, Crusader of the World, It's Not a Country, It's Winter*, and *Masada* and *Facts* (available in *Two Plays about Israel/Palestine*). He is a past resident playwright and artistic director of the Great Canadian Theatre Company in Ottawa, Canada, where he recently directed the world premiere of George F. Walker's *The Burden of Self-Awareness*. He is a featured columnist for *Inroads, the Canadian Journal of Opinion* (inroadsjournal.ca).

CPSIA information can be obtained
at www.ICGtesting.com
Printed in the USA
LVOW12s0102080716

495540LV00002B/2/P